Welcome to Your World, Baby

To my husband, Chris, who makes me laugh,
to my daughters, who make every day
more blessed than the one before,
and to my father, who would have laughed
so hard at these two funny little girls
—Brooke

For "Leah"
—Cori

Welcome to Your World, Baby

Text copyright © 2008 by Christa Inc   Illustrations copyright © 2008 by Cori Doerrfeld   Manufactured in China.   All rights reserved. No part of this book may be used or reproduced in any
manner whatsoever without written permission except in the case of brief quotations embodied in critical articles and reviews.   For information address HarperCollins Children's Books, a division of
HarperCollins Publishers, 1350 Avenue of the Americas, New York, NY 10019.   www.harpercollinschildrens.com   Library of Congress Cataloging-in-Publication Data is available.
ISBN 978-0-06-125311-9 (trade bdg.) — ISBN 978-0-06- 125312-6 (lib. bdg.)   Design by Stephanie Bart-Horvath   1 2 3 4 5 6 7 8 9 10 ❖ First Edition

Welcome to Your World, Baby

by Brooke Shields

illustrated by

Cori Doerrfeld

HarperCollinsPublishers

Welcome home, baby!
Welcome to your world.

This is your room.
I helped decorate it.

(I love pink!)

I help Mom wash you,
and you smell so sweet—
especially your feet.
I almost want to eat them,
but that would be silly!

This is my teddy bear,
but you can borrow him
until you are bigger and
aren't scared at night.

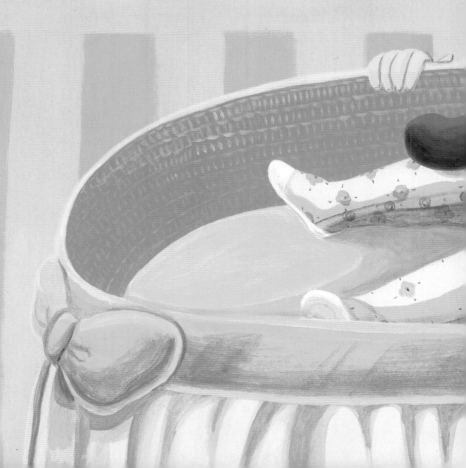

Soon we'll play
dress-up . . .

. . . and then put on a play.

I will be the princess.

And we'll end with a song.

Now that you are here,
we can have tea parties . . .

. . . and
super
secret
sleepovers.

We can play beauty parlor.

I'll have pink nail polish.
We can share.

I'll teach you your ABCs . . .

. . . and how to catch
snow with your tongue . . .

. . . and how to build
drip castles at the beach.

We can even share
cuddling with Mom.

I love being your big sister!